Goldilocks
and
the Three Bears

Illustrated by
Mike and Carl Gordon

Retold by Susanna Davidson

Once upon a time, there was a little girl called...

GOLDILOCKS!

She liked to do something naughty each day.

MONDAY...

TUESDAY...

WEDNESDAY...

..-.--.- Goldi

THURSDAY...

"Now..." thought Goldilocks. "What shall I do next?"

Goldilocks' mother always said, "Don't go into the forest. It's full of big, scary bears."

But Goldilocks wasn't scared.
So on Friday, she went into the forest.

"Ha!" she said.
"I can't see any bears."

She skipped happily along
the path until she saw...

...a pretty little cottage.

"I wonder who lives here?" thought Goldilocks, and went inside.

"Mmm..." she said.
On the table were three
delicious-smelling bowls of porridge.

"I'm sure no one would mind if I had a tiny taste,"
thought Goldilocks.

First, Goldilocks tried the great, big bowl.

Next, she tried the middle-sized bowl.

OW!
Too hot!

Last of all, Goldilocks
tried the tiny bowl.

"Yum! Yum!" she said.
"Just right!"

And she ate it ALL up.

Feeling full, Goldilocks looked for somewhere to sit.

First, she tried the great, big chair.

Too hard!

Next, she tried the middle-sized chair.

Too soft!

Last of all,
she tried the tiny chair.

"Aha!" thought Goldilocks.
"Just right." Until...

CRATK!

The chair broke.

"Oops!" said Goldilocks. "Time for a nap."

Upstairs, she found a great, big bed.

Too hard!

Next, she tried the middle-sized bed.

Too soft!

Last of all, she tried the tiny bed.
"Just right," said Goldilocks,
snuggling down.

Snore! Snore! Snore!

As she slept, a large paw
pulled open the front door.

Three bears plodded into the house.

There was...

a great big father bear,

a middle-sized mother bear

and a tiny little baby bear.

"Who's been eating *my* porridge?"
growled Father Bear.

"Who's been eating *my* porridge?" gasped Mother Bear.

"Who's been eating *my* porridge?" squeaked Baby Bear.

Father Bear looked around the room.

"Who's been sitting in *my* chair?" he growled.

"Well! Who's been sitting in *my* chair?" howled Mother Bear.

"Who's been sitting in *my* chair?" squeaked Baby Bear.

"They've broken it!"

They heard a rumbling "**snore**" coming from the bedroom.

The three bears climbed the stairs.

"Who's been sleeping in *my* bed?" growled Father Bear.

"Who's been sleeping in *my* bed?"
wailed Mother Bear.

"Who's been sleeping in *my* bed?"
squeaked Baby Bear.

"She's still there!"

Goldilocks woke up and
SCREAMED!

She flew out of the cottage and ran all the way home, crying...

"I'll NEVER, EVER be naughty again."

Nor did Goldilocks
EVER go into the
forest again.

Edited by Jenny Tyler and Lesley Sims
Designed by Caroline Spatz
Cover design by Louise Flutter

First published in 2008 by Usborne Publishing Ltd, 83-85 Saffron Hill, London EC1N 8RT, England.
www.usborne.com Copyright © 2008 Usborne Publishing Ltd. The name Usborne and the devices ⊕ ♔ are Trade Marks
of Usborne Publishing Ltd. All rights reserved. No part of this publication may be reproduced, stored in a retrieval system,
or transmitted in any form or by any means, electronic, mechanical, photocopying, recording or otherwise,
without the prior permission of the publisher. First published in America in 2008. UE. Printed in Dubai.